WILEY & GRAMPA'S CREATURE FEATURES

GRAMPA'S ZOMBIE BBQ

WRITTEN AND ILLUSTRATED BY

KIRK SCROGGS

LITTLE, BROWN AND COMPANY

New York · Boston · London

For Mama and Shmuggs

———

Special thanks to:
Ashley & Carolyn Grayson, Dan Hooker,
Suppasak Viboonlarp, Mark Mayes, Jackie Greed,
Rosa Jimenez, Joe Kocian, Amy Pennington, Alejandra,
Andrea, Sangeeta and Saho at Little, Brown
and Diane and Corey Scroggs.

Text and illustrations copyright © 2006 by Kirk Scroggs

Little, Brown and Company

Time Warner Book Group
1271 Avenue of the Americas, New York, NY 10020
Visit our Web site at www.lb-kids.com

First Edition: July 2006

Library of Congress Cataloging-in-Publication Data

Scroggs, Kirk.
   Grampa's Zombie BBQ/written and illustrated by Kirk Scroggs.—1st ed.
   p. cm.—(Wiley & Grampa's creature features; #2)
   Summary: When zombies show up at their annual barbecue, Wiley and Grampa try to
find a way to stop the hungry creatures from eating the other guests until Gramma comes
to the rescue with a surprise weapon.
   ISBN 0-316-05943-9 (hc)/ 0-316-05942-0 (pb)
   [1. Grandparents—Fiction. 2. Zombies—Fiction. 3. Humorous stories.] I. Title: Grampa's
zombie barbecue. II. Title.

PZ7.S436726Gra2006
[Fic]—dc22

2005044437

10 9 8 7 6 5 4 3 2 1

CW

Printed in the United States of America

Book design by Saho Fujii

The illustrations for this book were done in Staedtler ink on Canson Marker paper,
then digitized with Adobe Photoshop for color and shade.
The text was set in Humana Sans Light and the display type was hand lettered.

CHAPTERS

Let's Do Lunch

Ladies and gentlemen, friends, neighbors, and out-of-town guests . . . since the dawn of time, zombies have captivated the imaginations of sick individuals all over the globe. From the voodoo rituals of Zambowi Island to the classic zombie movies like *Night of the Brain Munchers* and *Benji Conquers the Zombies*.

But there is one more zombie tale to be told. A tale so horrifying that your spine will tingle, your toes will curl up in their socks, and your nose hairs will wiggle uncontrollably. This is the story of **Grampa's Zombie BBQ!**

We begin our story with a scene from the classic zombie film *Fried Spleen & Tomatoes*.

No, wait! That's just Vera, the Gingham County Elementary School lunch lady, dishing up some of her world-famous* Bulgarian sausage and sourcrowt goulash. (*World famous for causing uncontrollable upchucking, that is.)

That's me, Wiley, about to dig into some seriously stinky cuisine. And that guy next to me is Jubal, my best friend in all of Gingham County — besides Grampa, of course.

"This cafeteria should be declared a federal disaster area," I said, staring at my plate of pulsating slop.

"And Vera should be brought to justice for crimes against humanity," added Jubal.

Some folks say she performs voodoo rituals on her three bean and cabbage chili!

Others say she uses genuine skunk meat in her spicy Indonesian wontons!

And noted physicians say that her kidney bean and oatmeal pasta with BBQ sauce is not carb friendly!

CHAPTER 2

The Big Announcement

"BARBECUE SAUCE!" I shouted. "That reminds me!" Then I stood up and made a very important and dramatic announcement: "Children of Gingham Elementary, I beseech you! Drop those sporks and put down those chocolate milks!

"You're all invited to my grampa's annual barbecue tomorrow at 2:22 PM!

"There'll be games, sporting events, cold beverages and, of course, my gramma's prizewinning honey paprika barbecue sauce! That's right — real edible food! Not this tub of guts they call goulash! Oh . . . and please, everyone, bring a covered dish, preferably mayonnaise free."

The cafeteria erupted in cheers. This was going to be the best barbecue ever!

CHAPTER 3

Kid Science

Later that evening at Grampa's house, Channel 5's smarmy weatherman, Blue Norther, went on about some solar eclipse.

"Hi, folks! Blue Norther here. We've just gotten word from the Gingham County Observatory that tomorrow at 4:44 PM, there will be a total solar eclipse! It will be an amazing sight only seen once every few years! Just make sure, whatever you do, that you don't look at it! Staring at an eclipse could cause blindness, glaucoma, cataracts, or your eyeballs could burst into flames!"

Normally, Jubal and I would rush to the TV at the mere mention of eyeballs bursting into flames, but we were too busy with our science homework. We carefully mixed various ingredients and compounds under the strict adult supervision of Grampa. . . .

Actually, Grampa was napping.

"And now, I shall add the final ingredient to my secret compound," I announced.

"Wiley, maybe you shouldn't add the Tabasco sauce!" Jubal warned. "I've got a bad feeling."

"NONSENSE, MY DEAR BOY!" I said defiantly. "What if Thomas Edison hadn't added the Tabasco sauce? We wouldn't have light bulbs today! What if Sir Isaac Newton hadn't added the Tabasco sauce?"

"No Fig Newtons?" asked Jubal.

"Precisely!" I said.

CHAPTER 4

Don't Try This at Home!

And if I hadn't added the Tabasco sauce . . .

that huge fireball wouldn't have shot over our heads . . .

soared across the room . . .

and landed on Grampa's unsuspecting foot,
which went up in flames like a batch of dried
twigs!

"It's nothing, Grampa," I said nervously. "Go back to sleep."

Needless to say, Gramma was none too pleased. "I will not have dangerous chemical experiments in this house!" she bellowed. "What if that fireball had hit my new drapes instead of Grampa's foot?!"

GRAMMA'S
ANGER METER
(CURRENTLY AT BURNT ORANGE)

GINGHAM COUNTY CASSEROLE QUEEN '95

Gramma forced us to dispose of our new
compound, which I called PPK.

"It stands for Plutonium Powder Keg," I
declared. "Jubal, we must hide this dangerous
yet important formula where no human hands
will touch it." So we hid it high on a shelf in the
shed out in the backyard.

CHAPTER 5

Morning Marinade

The next morning at 6 AM, Gramma was already up trying out her new Super Marinade 5000. "Wow, check out Gramma!" I said.

"I've got 375 chickens and 53 yards of sausage to marinade with my honey paprika barbecue sauce!" said Gramma as she hosed down the chickens. "That's the secret to my barbecue — lots of paprika! — Paprika, paprika, paprika!"

While Gramma prepared the poultry, Merle and I tested out the Slick 'n' Slide to make sure it was at the proper slickness.

Then I helped Grampa fire up the behemoth George Porkin Megagrill XE, which Grampa ignited by remote control, for fear of singeing his other foot.

"OOOOOH! I ALMOST FORGOT!" yelled Gramma. "Don't forget to make the lemonade!"

"IT'S ALL RIGHT, GRANNY!" said Grampa.
"Merle's mixin' it as we speak!"

By 2:30 PM, most of the guests had arrived and the party was hoppin'.

The delicious smell of BBQ brought visitors in from all over Gingham County.

At 3:00 we held our usual Watermelon Seed Spitting Championship. Gramma finds this quite disgusting.

Then it was time for Extreme Horseshoe Tossing.

At 4:00 we had our annual Gingham County Deaf Jam Poetry Reading (my least favorite BBQ activity).

And at 4:44 the local branch of Heck's Angels were in the middle of a mean game of volleyball with the Sisters of No Mercy when . . .

CHAPTER 7

There Goes the Sun

Suddenly, the sky went dark as an ominous shadow covered the sun. It was the eclipse! Blue Norther was right!

"OH, FIDDLE!" complained Gramma, sporting her new swimsuit. "I was ready to tan!"

"Well, this stinks," I said. "Maybe today isn't such a good day for a barbecue."

"Never fear, Wiley," said Grampa. "A little electromagnetic interference won't ruin our party. Besides, what else could go wrong?"

He had to ask.

Vera, the lunch lady, showed up with 27 gallons of her spicy beet borscht (that's ice-cold beet soup, for the uninformed). Everyone gasped and youngsters hid under the picnic tables.

"STOP!" I said. "Halt! Alto! I'm sorry. No further guests are permitted on the property! We have reached capacity. Besides, that borscht is considered a toxic substance by the League of Human Decency!" (I have to admit, I made that last bit up.)

"But . . . you said everyone who brought a covered dish was invited," said Vera, softly shedding a solitary tear.

SOLITARY TEAR

STOP

"AND HE MEANT IT!" interrupted Grampa. "Of course you're invited! Wiley, where are your manners? Get this poor woman some refreshments and go put this borscht in the garage with the other dangerous chemicals!"

CHAPTER 8
Uninvited Guests

Just when things couldn't get any worse, Old
Man Copperthwaite, the crazy gravedigger,
came running and screaming like a banshee,
"They're a comin'! The zombies are a comin'!
They popped out of their graves and they're
headed this way! Hundreds of 'em!"

"Hundreds of them?" said Gramma.
"I hope they bring covered dishes!"

Sure enough, all of the residents of Eternal
Naps Cemetery were crawling out of their
graves and coming down the hill!

A virtual army of the undead was heading our way, and they sure looked hungry.

"DON'T PANIC!" Grampa assured the guests. "Everyone stay calm! There is nothing to fear! Zombies are people, just like you and me . . . except, of course, they've returned from the grave to eat our vital organs and perhaps gnaw on our bones a bit and maybe chew on our toes like jellybeans . . . but other than that, there is nothing to fear!"

The zombies got closer and closer, drooling and licking their rotten chops.

Our guests were getting nervous and I had to prevent a panic.

"DON'T WORRY, FOLKS!" I shouted. "We have guard hounds! They'll protect us!"

But Esther and Chavez were already bunkered in.

CHAPTER 9

The Not-So-Final Showdown

"OH, WELL!" I shouted, pulling out my slingshot. "It's up to us to fight the zombie menace! Citizens of Gingham County, arm yourselves!"

Gramma whipped out her kitchen arsenal.

The nuns struck their Praying Mantis stance.

Grampa napped!

The zombies slowly lumbered in and attacked!

"Oh, I can't stand it!" Jubal cried, covering his face with his hands. "The crunching of bones! The munching and smacking sounds of zombies eating our friends and neighbors! Oh, the humanity!"

"Wait a minute," I interrupted, "you can stop your wimpering, Jubal! The zombies are eating the barbecue! They must have smelled Gramma's delicious honey paprika sauce!"

"I'LL BE!" said Gramma.

"Wow, Granny!" exclaimed Grampa. "Your cooking usually sends people to their graves, not the other way around!"

CHAPTER 10

How to Entertain Zombies

So the zombies ate chicken and sausage and ate and ate, as fast as Grampa could grill. "Grampa," I said, " this is shaping up to be the weirdest barbecue ever!"

"You know you're right, Wiley," agreed Grampa, "even weirder than the Great Sack Race Collision of 1987!"

And things just got weirder. . . .

Jubal got into a doozy of a tetherball match with Julius R. Gingham, our town founder, who had unsuccessfully wrestled a rabid coyote in 1862.

Gramma shared beauty secrets with the Ladies' Quilting League, lost in the Great Blizzard of 1912.

No BBQ would be complete without zombie karaoke (earplugs recommended).

And we held what had to be the world's first zombie sack race!

"These zombies may not talk much," said Grampa, "but they're courteous and gracious guests. Who would've thought that we'd be dining with legendary cowboy Wild Bill Hiccup and his wife?"

Grampa was right. Most people would think eating with a zombie would be pretty disgusting, but that just wasn't the case . . .

except for when Wild Bill's nose fell into the potato salad.

CHAPTER 11

A Vord of Varning!

"Ze zombie's appetite can never be satisfied!"
came an eerie voice from the inflatable pool. It
was Dr. Hans Lotion and his grandson, Jurgen.
"Zey vill eat and eat and ven zey run out of
food, zey vill eat vatever zey can get zeir
zombie hands on! Zey vill eat anything!"

"Anything?" I asked, a little worried.

"Vell, almost anyzing," said Hans. "You know ze little vite chunks in ze pork 'n' beans? Even zombies vill not eat zat."

"So why have they returned from the grave?" asked Gramma.

"Could be anyzing," said Hans. "Ze Solar eclipse, global varming, ze smell of your delicious honey paprika sauce. Ve may never know. Vat I do know is zis, ve must appease ze zombies' appetites or suffer grave consequences!"

CHAPTER 12

Uh-Oh Part I

Nate Farkles made a poorly timed announcement at that moment. "Sorry, folks. We're out of barbecue!"

An eerie silence fell over the party as the zombies stared at us, drooling. "Be very still, Wiley," Grampa whispered. "Whatever you do, don't make any moves that might seem hostile or appetizing in any way."

CHAPTER 13

Total Chaos

Then the zombies went berserk and attacked
the side dishes!

They devoured all
92 pounds of potato
salad . . .

gnawed their way
through forty-six
ears of corn . . .

and wolfed down 54 pounds of baked beans,
which created a whole new explosive situation!

TOOL SHED

PLEASE
KNOCK
BEFORE
ENTERING

When the beans were gone, the zombies came
after *us*!

"I don't want to alarm anyone,"
shouted Grampa,
"but our gassy zombie guests
are still hungry!
Run for your lives!"

Some of the guests ran off into the woods.

The nuns, being natural climbers, headed for Grampa's big oak.

"LOOK, GRAMPA!" I shouted as we crowded into the house. "Heck's Angels are running away! Aren't bikers supposed to be tough?"

"I SHOULD HAVE KNOWN!" said Grampa. "Real bikers don't ride electric scooters!"

CHAPTER 14

Trapped!

Inside the house, we boarded everything up.
"LOOK!" said Gramma, pointing at the TV.
"Blue Norther is about to make an emergency
announcement!"

We all waited in hushed silence.

"Hi, folks! Blue Norther here at the 51st annual Betty Crockpot Bake-Off, where I'm standing with Minnie Purvis, the grand prize winner! Not only has Minnie brought us a sample of her delicious Baked Nebraska with butter-creme filling, but she's agreed to share the ingredients to this delicious dish with our viewers right now!"

"Zombies are attacking and that's his emergency news?" I griped.

"And they call this journalism," complained Grampa.

"I gotta write this down," said Gramma. "This is good stuff!"

Suddenly, the zombies casually strolled in through the back door, which had been left unlocked!

CHAPTER 15

Up Yonder!

"QUICK!" I yelled. "Everybody run upstairs, where there's absolutely no chance of escape!"

All twenty-seven of us piled into Grampa and
Gramma's bedroom, and we blocked the door
with Gramma's collection of romance novels.

"Well," announced Grampa, "that should keep
them out for at least ten minutes!"

CHAPTER 16

The Blame Game

"Why is this happening?" asked our hysterical neighbor Loretta Cartwright. "Why are zombies roaming Gingham County?"

"It's the solar eclipse!" shouted old man Romero.

"I think it was something in that barbecue!"
said Betty Hubris. Gramma found this statement
particularly hurtful.

"NONSENSE!" I interrupted. "There is a perfectly
logical reason for what's happened. It's all her
fault! Vera, the lunch lady! The second she
arrived, everything went haywire! She's evil . . .
evil!!!"

"WILEY!" bellowed Gramma, her anger meter in the red. "I am ashamed of you! Don't you know it's not polite to blame the dead rising from their graves on a dinner guest?"

I must admit, I felt a little silly.

All of a sudden, a meow for help caught our
attention and we rushed to the window!

"Oh no!" shouted Gramma. "Merle's trapped in the garden shed and the zombies are coming for him!"

CHAPTER 17

Dead Bug Walkin'!

Merle was securing his minicompound when an eerie buzz came from above. It was the bug zapper, glowing a ghastly blue.

To make matters worse, the dried dead bugs
under the zapper were getting up and walking!
And they were coming for Merle!

"Kitty! Kitty!" buzzed the dried bug zombies as they closed in on Merle for their cat dinner.

"OH, I CAN'T WATCH!" cried Gramma.

"Don't worry, Honey," comforted Grampa. "Just think of it this way, you'll never find another hairball in your fluffy slippers ever again!"

CHAPTER 18

To the Rescue

"I can't just sit back and watch!" I yelled bravely. "I've got a plan to rescue Merle! All I need is a pair of Gramma's finest and strongest panty hose!"

"I always knew that boy was talented!" said Grampa.

So Jubal and I grabbed a pair of Gramma's stockings and shimmied down to the shed while the hungry zombies clutched at our feet.

We burst into the shed to find . . . Merle had
pulled the old reverse-bug-munch trick and was
picking little hairy bug legs out of his teeth.

"MEEEOOOOWWWUURRRPPP!" said Merle.
(That's cat for "Burp!")

"That's pretty sick," said Jubal.

CHAPTER 19

Secret Weapon

We were just about to escape the shed when I suddenly remembered our explosive compound up on the top shelf.

"I KNOW!" I shouted. "While we're down here, let's grab the PPK! Maybe we can use it against the zombies!"

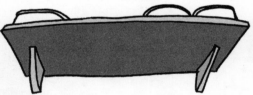

CHAPTER 20

Uh-Oh Part II

So we formed a human-feline ladder to boost me up to the shelf so I could grab the secret . . .

"HEY! IT'S GONE!" I yelled. "All I see up here is a bunch of paprika!"

Paprika? Suddenly, I had a very, very bad feeling.

My mind raced as I recalled the events leading up to the zombie attack.

"I shall call it PPK!"

"I'll put it high on the shelf where no human hands will get to it!"

"That's the secret to my barbecue!— Lots of paprika!— **Paprika, paprika, paprika!**"

"UH-OH!" I said gloomily.

So we shimmied back up to the bedroom to deliver the bad news.

"Boy," I said, panting, "this is a lot harder going up!"

"I wish I hadn't eaten five plates of barbecue!" complained Jubal.

Gramma was so happy to be reunited with Merle that she gave him a big bear hug.

"Careful, Granny," warned Grampa, "that cat's already survived one near-death experience!"

CHAPTER 21

An Embarrassing Confession

"Ladies and gentlemen," I announced, "I'm afraid I have an embarrassing confession to make. . . ."

"That's a good idea, Wiley," Grampa interrupted. "Because we soon will most likely be devoured by zombies, I too have something I'd like to get off my chest. Something that now, in our final moments, I have come to terms with: I am a life-time member of the Pippi Longstocking Fan Club. I also bite my toenails and sleep with a teddy bear named Shmuggles."

CHAPTER 22

Not That Embarrassing!

"No, no, no," I broke in, "Jubal and I have done something horrible! We created a chemical compound so powerful it blew up Grampa's foot! And that's not all! We accidentally hid the compound on Gramma's spice rack in the shed!"

"What are you saying?" asked Gramma.

"I'm saying that our compound made its way into your barbecue sauce and that could be the reason why its delicious aroma woke the dead!"

Gramma went off like Mount Krakatoa! "You mean to tell me," she fumed, "that because of you, I put a highly volatile chemical in my beloved barbecue . . . one that explodes—"

"THAT'S IT!" I interrupted her tirade. "Our compound explodes when combined with Tabasco sauce! If we could douse the zombies with the stuff, we could blow 'em up! But where do we get enough Tabasco?"

"My spicy beet borscht is 82 percent Tabasco," offered Vera the lunch lady, "but you locked it in the garage."

I was so happy I could have kissed her (but I didn't). "We've got to get to that borscht!" I exclaimed. "If only we had something we could distract the zombies with to get to the garage!"

"I've got just the thing," said Grampa as he pushed a button on his universal remote. Just then, Gramma's portrait of Elvis opened up to reveal a monster stash of Pork Cracklins!

"Succulent deep-fried pig skins to distract the zombies!"

"Why would you need this many Pork Cracklins?" asked Gramma, still angry.

"In case of World War III," said Grampa, embarrassed, "or a pork shortage."

CHAPTER 23

The Plan Comes Together

So I laid out my plan. "Grampa and I will use the Pork Cracklins to draw the zombies away from the house!"

"Meanwhile, Jubal and Nate will disguise themselves as zombies and make their way to the garage, grab the borscht, and then we'll dump it on the zombies!"

Gramma and her Ladies' Quilting League friends knitted us suits made out of Pork Cracklins.

Grampa and I squeezed in a power workout to beef up for our dangerous mission.

The Reverend Moe said a prayer for us. "Protect these crazy fools. And if they are caught by the zombies, let their deaths be quick and relatively painless!"

Finally, we used Gramma's avocado and cucumber face mask to turn Jubal and Nate into zombies.

We were ready. The game was afoot!

CHAPTER 24

The Not-So-Great Escape

Grampa and I burst into the crowded hallway in our Pork Cracklins suits. We quickly ran for the stairs.

"COME AND GET IT, YOU FILTHY ZOMBIE SWINE!" yelled Grampa. "All you can eat grampa and grandson! The boy tastes just like chicken, and I taste like aged angus beef! And did I mention, we're covered in pork rinds?"

While Grampa taunted the zombies, Jubal and Nate snuck out and silently slipped in with the zombies, unnoticed.

"Yuck!" grimaced Jubal, dripping with avocado face cream. "This stuff is gross!"

"I kinda like it," exclaimed Nate. "My pores are tingling and my skin has never felt so young!"

Grampa and I made it out the front door and
took off across the yard. But the zombies were
gaining on us!

Just as the zombies were about to catch us, we
made it to the Slick 'n' Slide and slid out of their
rotten zombie grasps. (It should be noted that
zombies are notoriously afraid of open flame,
the metric system, and Slick 'n' Slides.)

"OH, NO!" I screamed, looking back toward the house.

"Jubal and Nate are aborting the mission!"

It seemed that the zombies had smelled the avocado face cream and were chasing Jubal and Nate with tortilla chips.

"Sorry, guys!" yelled Nate. "Who knew zombies were partial to guacamole?"

"We've got to get braver friends," complained Grampa.

CHAPTER 25

Uh-Oh Part III

We turned and tried to escape, but we ran smack dab into Gramma's cactus garden. There was nowhere to go. We were trapped like Pork Cracklin-covered rats.

"Well," said Grampa as the zombies closed in on us, "this is it, Wiley. The end of the road! I only wish we could have lived long enough to eat these suits!"

CHAPTER 26

It's Raining Borscht!

"HEY, ZOMBIES!" yelled a voice from the hill. It was Gramma. Apparently, while the zombies were chasing us, she had slipped out the back and grabbed her Super Marinade 5000 . . . and better yet, she had filled it with Vera's borscht!

"Soup's on!" Gramma yelled as she hosed the zombies down with the toxic borscht.

"Just beet it!" she remarked as she slathered more of our undead guests.

"How 'bout another serving?" she remarked as she sprayed the last of the zombies.

And, just as I had predicted, the zombies reacted explosively with the borscht and ran away, which was good because Gramma was almost out of borscht *and* witty one-liners.

CHAPTER 27

Adios!

The zombies, outwitted by beet soup and Pork Cracklins, ran back home to the cemetery.

"And next year, don't show up unless you're invited!" yelled Gramma.

"You know, Wiley," said Grampa, "if it weren't for the awful stench and the fact that they tried to eat us, those zombies wouldn't be half bad! I think I might invite them back for spaghetti night!"

CHAPTER 28

Epilogue of the Living Dead

So that's my story, folks! Everything turned out peachy keen. Gramma and Vera were declared heroes.

Vera's borscht was purchased by the government for study and possible military use.

Gramma's story was turned into a hit
action movie.

As for our secret compound, Jubal and I decided
to bury it in a secure location . . .

deep in the woods, where it could cause no
further harm to humanity.

Oh well,
at least we tried.

What's up with Jubal's camera? He took two shots of the Zombie Karaoke Sing-Off, but there's something about the second picture that just doesn't seem right. Can you pick out the differences between the two pictures, or are we just crazy?

The answers are on the next page. Anyone caught cheating will be fed to the zombies with a tangy honey mustard sauce!